THE GHOSTBUSTERS

Lost and Foundry

Maureen Spurgeon

CARNIVAL

"Fire!" Peter Venkman shouted. "The foundry ghost is right over there!"

Ion beams from four Proton Guns whizzed across the deserted ironworks. There was an explosion, the sound of breaking glass, and a giant sign shattered into tiny pieces, crashing to the ground.

There was a moment's silence, before a wailing scream pierced the air, and a hideous, glowing blob with the ugliest face any of the Ghostbusters had ever seen lunged towards them.

"Out of the way!" yelled Egon Spengler.

"I thought I'd got him!" snapped Peter, most annoyed.

"Where's he gone, now?" wondered Ray Stantz. "Let's have a Psycho Kinetic Energy Reading, Egon!"

"One moment, while I consult my PKE meter!" Egon announced, sounding very learned. "He must be around, somewhere!"

"This way!" he bawled, running along a passage-way stacked with piles of coal on one side and iron on the other.

Winston gave an excited yelp.

"There he is, now! Right over that vat of molten steel!"

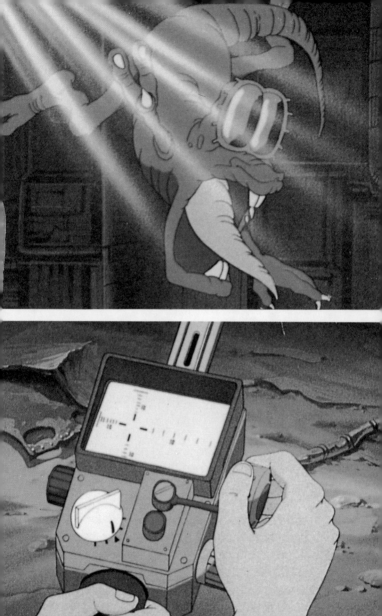

At the same moment as the ion beams from four Proton Guns streaked towards the ghost, the huge bucket slid along the cable overhead. It stopped, then tipped itself over, the ghost completely disappearing behind a shower of molten steel pouring into the vat below.

"Where did he go?" wondered Winston, after a pause. "We hardly had time to hit him!"

"There's no reading on the PKE meter, either." Egon was clearly puzzled. "Could he have simply--- vanished?"

"Come on, you guys . . ." Peter Venkman had just about had enough. "I reckon we've seen the last of that ghost, anyway!"

The Ghostbusters' Ectomobile sped away into the distance, nobody noticing that some girders on a fork lift truck were glowing with a ghostly gleam . . .

Anyone passing the Ghostbusters' HQ might think it looked like an old Fire Station. And, they'd be right. The alarm bell which once summoned firemen now rang for the Ghostbusters to spring into action, sliding down the fireman's pole, ready to leap into their ectomobile which was parked where fire engines had once stood.

But, all a down-to-earth Ghostbuster like Winston Zeddmore wanted was a warm shower and a change of clothes. Too bad that somebody – or, rather, something – had got into his locker, slopping a splodge of green slime right on to Winston's shirt with a loud SPLAT!

"Slimer . . ." groaned Winston, fingering the shirt gingerly. "Say, why do we have to have our own ghost, living here with us? And why is he wearing my uniform?"

"Because he really wants to be a Ghostbuster?" Ray Stantz guessed, slipping off his Proton Pack. "Doesn't Winston's uniform suit the little guy, fellas?"

"He looks real cute!" growled Peter Venkman. He had never forgiven Slimer for getting him on his first job.

Slimer was rather upset, idly picking up Ray's gun from the Proton Pack on the floor, pulling the trigger and thinking how unjust life was . . .

"Hey!" shouted Peter. "Slimer, leave that alone!"

But the ion beams had already hit the fireman's pole in the centre of the room, splitting it into two blackened, twisted halves.

"Now we need a new pole!" sighed Egon – once Peter had finished raging and cursing. "Get on the

phone to the ironworks, will you, Janine?"

The biggest department store in the neighbourhood was having problems, too.

"A refrigerator, gone missing?" the manager thundered at his assistant. "What do you mean?"

"It – it was here a minute ago, sir . . ." the man hardly knew what to say. "And, then---"

There was a low hum, then the whine of a refrigerator being switched on, swelling into a roar loud enough to fill the entire store.

"I – I don't believe it!" the manager gasped in horror. "I just don't believe it . . ."

For there, right in front of his eyes, was the refrigerator, rocking clumsily towards him, its twin doors opening and closing like enormous, square jaws.

"Aaaagh---!" he screamed as he was showered by a barrage of ice cubes. "Quick! Somebody, call in the Ghostbusters!"

The manager was still pale and shaking when our heroes arrived at the store, long after the refrigerator had been and gone.

"What was it like?" asked Venkman, leading the Ghostbusters through long rows of refrigerators. What model did you say it was?"

"No-Frost, No-Ice – and with twin doors!" The manager gave another shudder.

"Avocado green!" his assistant added.

"Well, here's the space where it was," said Winston pointing. "What about that puddle of melted ice on the floor, Ray?"

"No readings on the PKE meter!" replied Stantz, flicking a few switches.

"Nothing on the Plasmatometer, either," added Spengler. "You know, this could be nothing more than a faulty refrigerator . . ."

Meanwhile, further along the street, workmen had arrived to lay cable for the latest T.V. channel.

"Wow!" one of the men panted. "This new cable feels extra heavy!" The words were barely out of his mouth when the cable whipped towards him, hard enough to hurl him clean into the air. "Hey!" he shrieked out. "What's happening here?"

"Help!" he screamed. "Ghostbusters!"

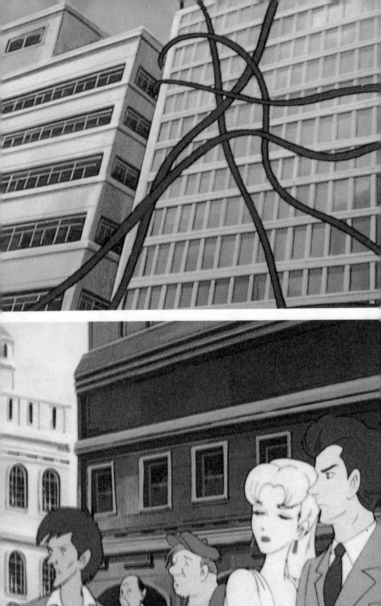

Peter Venkman was in no mood for polite talk by the time ECTO 1 arrived at the scene.

"Okay," he grunted. "So, where's this ghost of yours?"

"Peter!" shouted Ray. "Get down!"

And before anyone else could say another word, the cable had sliced through a tree, leaving the Ghostbusters and the workmen sprawled out on the pavement.

"Any more questions?" demanded one workman, yelling to make himself heard above the roar of the tree crashing down.

"You ain't seen nothing, yet!" his friend added darkly.

Peter was soon considering this to be an understatement. Thousands of feet of heavy steel cable had become looped through an entire building, threading itself in and out of windows, tangled knots dangling like bunches of grapes.

"The thing's gone haywire!" yelled Spengler. "Look at the end of that cable, it's just waving in the air!"

"And winding itself into a spinning lasso!" screamed Winston. "Get out the Proton Guns, before it gets us!"

The whole building reddened and glowed as the Ghostbusters fired their ion beams, the cable first shrinking back into a tight coil, then crashing into the street below and disappearing down a manhole.

"It's getting away!" shouted Winston.

"Well," said Peter firmly. "I'm not going after it!"

For one young man working in a hardware store, the day had begun just like any other. He certainly was not expecting a box of nails to jump straight out of his hands as he was stacking them on a shelf!

"Hey----!" he burst out. But the box had already hit the floor and split open, nails spilling out and scattering everywhere, then gathering in formation and flying out of the door like a great swarm of bees.

"Nails!" screamed the terrified customers, dashing out into the street in a fit of panic. "Get away from those nails!"

The Ghostbusters heard them in their Ectomobile, three blocks away.

"Sounds like more trouble," Winston predicted wearily. "Proton Packs on again, I reckon!"

At first, all they could see was a store with the name "MR. HAMMER", and the words "BIG NAIL SALE" painted on the front. Then came the sound of the large, plate glass window being shattered, and a mass of nails smashed out into the air, whizzing along like a jet plane.

"Get down!" shouted Zeddmore. "They're heading our way!"

There was a thunderous roar, and the ragged shadow of a black cloud of nails passing right overhead. Then, one by one, the Ghostbusters lifted their heads.

"They almost nailed us that time," said Peter Venkman with a smile.

Not too far away, the manager of a supermarket was busily arranging cans of peas into an impressive pyramid.

The pyramid began to wobble precariously. It felt as if a can near the very bottom of the pile was being snatched by someone doing their shopping in a tearing hurry.

"On, no!" the manager burst out. "Please, don't touch----"

CRASH! The entire pyramid of peas collapsed to the ground in a sprawling heap. Dozens of cans began rolling towards the manager, making him shrink back in terror.

"Aaaagh---!" he shrieked, fleeing into the street – just as the Ghostbusters' Ectomobile came into sight. "The cans are chasing me!"

"Oh, boy!" sighed Peter Venkman. "Ever had one of those days?"

"The cans are heading for that alley-way, Peter!" shouted Ray. "We'll have to get out and follow them!"

"They've come up against a brick wall!" yelled Winston, coming up to the entrance.

"And there's no other way out!" pronounced Peter with a grin. "Anyone got a tin opener?"

Nobody answered him. Everyone could see that the cans had begun to roll themselves up and over the wall.

"Well!" said Ray, quick-thinking as usual. "Those weren't ordinary cans!"

And in another part of town, a brand-new, modern statue was about to be unveiled before an audience of most distinguished art-lovers.

"My new sculpture explores vast avenues of expression!" the lady artist was droning on. "I call it anti-neo-post-modernism!"

The people held their breath.

"Oh, yes!" the woman nodded, most gratified. "I think you must agree, the effect of my new creation is quite startling!"

She never spoke a truer word. At that moment, the sculpture was rising high into the air with the white cloth still draped over it, looking like a Hallowe'en ghost. Then, with a graceful elegance, the statue seemed to shake itself, the cloth fluttering to the ground.

There was a frenzy of wild, high-pitched screams,

as the statue raised itself to its full height, pawing the air like a giant horse, almost neighing with the sound of grating metal, before it galloped away, leaving its creator in a dead faint on the ground.

The screams and cries of terror from the crowd almost drowned out the wailing siren on the Ghostbusters' Ectomobile.

"Now, what's wrong?" groaned Peter, holding tight to the steering wheel. "Looks like some kind of strange horse, gone crazy!"

"You can say that again!" agreed Egon. "And it looks like it's made of steel, like the other things."

"Watch out for that bus straight ahead!" Winston was already diving down in his seat, but the peculiar-looking steel sculpture seemed determined to keep going, clearing the bus in one single leap, as if it were the champion hurdler in a steeplechase.

It looked as though the same artist might have had something to do with the design of a new, modern skyscraper being built close by. Only two building workers sitting on a girder made it look anything like normal.

"What's in your lunch box today?" asked one, an upright girder casting a long, thin shadow across his safety helmet. "Anything special?"

"No, looks like the same old thing!" his friend complained, unaware that the girder was moving closer. "D'you like peanut butter?"

The first workman would have given a polite answer – if the girder hadn't bumped into him and knocked him off his seat. As it was, all he could do was scream "No-o-o-o!" as he fell.

The whole city seemed to be teetering on the brink of some mad disaster.

"Refrigerators. . . cables. . . nails. . . cans, and now girders. . . all gone haywire," mused Egon. "Things all made out of steel. . . "

His thoughts were interrupted by a shout from Ray.

"Over there! See those girders, sort of crawling out of the building like they were great big slugs?"

"One of them's winding around that column supporting the skyscraper!" boomed Peter. "Let's get at it!"

It only took a moment for the ion beams from all four Proton Guns to whizz through the air, blasting away not only the cables, but the columns with them.

Without any columns to support it, the skyscraper began to topple forward, crumbling apart, section by section, until there was one huge, thundering roar as bricks, masonry, great slabs of concrete, iron and steel hurtled to the ground in a great cloud of dust, right in the path of the four Ghostbusters.

Amazingly, nobody was hurt. The Ghostbusters found themselves sheltered by the central circle of stone, staring around dazedly at the ruins surrounding them.

But, from the bottom of a giant pile of twisted steel, two girders crawled out like two enormous earthworms. . .

As the Ghostbusters patrolled the city, reports were coming in of everything from scissors to washing machines taking walks through the streets. A gang of hooligans dived into a police station screaming that they'd been attacked by flying hub-caps when they tried breaking into a car. One policeman said he could have sworn he saw a refrigerator rocking its way towards a busy traffic underpass, closely followed by cans of peas, swarms of nails, and a set of speeding hub-caps.

As for that modern piece of sculpture which the artist had been so proud of — that had decided to gallop off on its own. It rather liked the look of a particular scrap-yard. . .

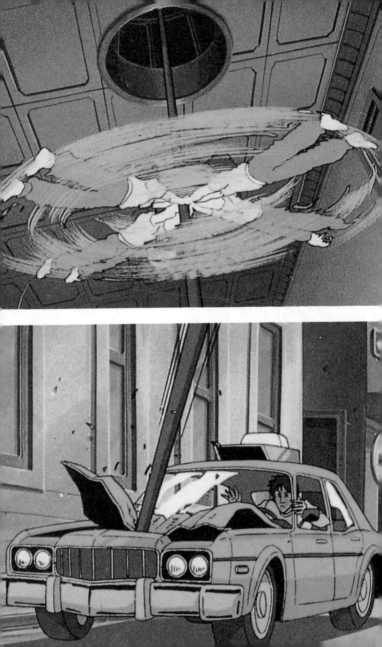

"The new fireman's pole's been fitted!" greeted Janine, as the Ghostbusters staggered into their H.Q. "Oh, yes – and there's been a call to say a refrigerator's trying to cross six lanes of traffic!"

"Here we go again," groaned Peter. "Good thing we've got this new po-o-o-ole-- aaaagh!"

Instead of sliding to the ground floor, Peter began spinning around the pole so fast he became a blur.

"Peter!" Egon rapped out. "Stop fooling around!"

"Who's fooling?" Peter demanded, shooting up and down the pole like a yo-yo. "Get me off this thing!"

They all tugged at his legs, ending up in a heap on the floor with Venkman on top. Meanwhile the pole was bending double, wrenching out the bolts which held it to the floor!

"That pole came from the ironworks," said Ray at last. "The ion beams from our Proton Guns must have fused that ghost in with the molten steel."

"That refrigerator. . . " faltered Winston. "The nails, the girders---- they're all part of the same ghost?"

"Yeah – so if that's true wouldn't all the different parts try getting back together?" persisted Ray.

With an ear-shattering din, the new fireman's pole shot out of the window like a huge arrow, bouncing away down the street.

Next moment, the Ghostbusters were chasing
right behind in the Ectomobile, skidding to a stop
when the bouncing pole disappeared behind an
enormous heap of twisted, rusty metal in a very
cluttered scrap-yard.

There was a loud series of clanks and rumbles.
Gleaming hub caps rose up from the heart of the
pile. Then a refrigerator mouth, then a boiler body
rising up on its girder legs, towering high above the
Ghostbusters. All the different parts of the ghost had
come together to form a monstrous metal monster.

Proton Guns fired. The monster gave a roar like
the sound of grinding gears, grating metal and
banging pipes. Peter Venkman gave a whoop of
triumph.

"There goes a girder leg, Ray!"

"But it's joining on again, as an arm!" Stantz

pointed out in panic. "See? And our fireman's pole is the leg!"

The creature began coming towards them with slow, giant steps, still roaring loudly the whole time.

"Dodge behind the next stack of cars!" hissed Winston. "I'm going to try the remote pedal on my Ghost Trap!"

The creature couldn't work out what had happened. He looked all around for the Ghostbusters. Ray held his breath.

"Now!" Zeddmore burst out at last, stepping on the remote pedal. The trap doors flew open.

"Grrrr---!" bellowed the monster, trampling on Winston's Ghost Trap with one mighty foot, then proceeding to knock down whole piles of wrecked cars with a single sweep of its enormous hand.

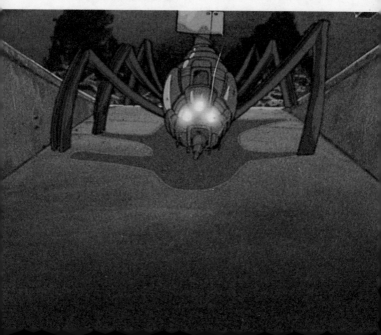

"Into the car crusher, straight ahead!" shouted Ray Stantz. "It's the only way!"

With another terrifying roar, the monster came after the Ghostbusters, all four racing out the other side of the car crusher ahead of the slow, ponderous steps of the steel creature chasing them.

Looking pleased with himself, Stantz pressed a red button. The low whine of the machinery began overpowering the steely roars of the ghost monster – until, at last, it was nothing more than a small cube of tightly compressed metal.

Not for long, though. The cube rapidly began unfolding, soon becoming a flat, monster-size square, chasing the Ghostbusters twice as fast as it had before!

"Quick!" yelled Winston, diving towards the cab of an electro-magnetic crane. "In here!"

In desperation, he fumbled around, pushing and pulling levers, but hardly knowing what he was doing.

Then suddenly, the huge arm of the crane crashed down on to the monster, metal pieces scattering all over the ground – but instantly joining together again, clanging and crashing into yet another ghostly steel creature, even uglier than the other two!

The Ghostbusters knew they had to get out of the crane to escape, but Venkman had further troubles.

"Help!" he yelled out. "Help! I'm trapped here by a cable on my Proton Pack!"

"Hold on, Peter!" cried Winston. "We're coming!"

But the metal monster had got there first, grabbing the crane with its gigantic steel claws whilst Venkman tugged hard at his Proton Pack.

"Look!" shouted Stantz.

The huge electro magnet at the end of the crane had begun swinging to the vibrations of a loud, electrical hum coming from Venkman's Proton Gun. Drawn by the magnet, a few bits shot out from the monster, the creature hurling itself after the loose parts. Within seconds, it had crashed into the giant magnet, more of its pieces falling apart, leaving only a mass of scrap metal.

The jumbled pieces of the steel monster were still stuck to the magnet when Peter drove the crane back to the ironworks, Winston sat beside him in the cab.

Venkman drove the crane inside the foundry.

"Steady does it---" warned Winston, watching Peter's hands on the control levers. "We want to get that magnet right over the vat of hot metal!"

"Now. . . " breathed Venkman, pressing a button to de-electrolyse the magnet.

There was a burst of loud splashes and hisses as, one by one, piece by piece, the parts from the metal monster fell into the molten steel.

"Okay, so far," Winston murmered. "Now, pick up our Ghost Trap with the crane arm, Peter."

The rest was fairly easy. The Ghost Trap swung over the vat, there was a rude belch from the bubbling hot steel – and up popped the foundry ghost, just as the Ghostbusters has first seen him. He was sucked into the Ghost Trap before he even knew what was happening.

Peter gave a loud cheer.

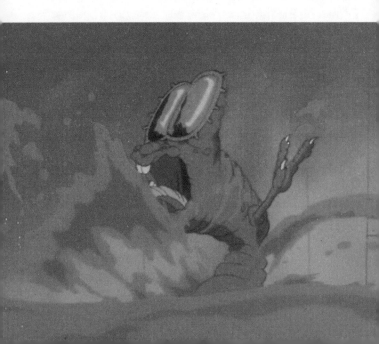

With the magnet working up and down and back and forth as Venkman experimented with the controls, Ray and Egon exchanged long suffering glances.

"Don't you just love this thing, Winston? How about getting one for Janine back at Ghostbusters' HQ?"

Later back at HQ, Ray asks the question:

"You don't think he wants to buy one, do you Egon?"

Egon began cleaning his spectacles. "Well," he reasoned, "If he does, we'll never have to worry about lost paper clips ever again!"

Carnival
An imprint of the Children's Division
of the Collins Publishing Group
8 Grafton Street, London W1X 3LA

Published by Carnival 1988
Reprinted 1989

ISBN 0 00 194439 8

Printed & bound in Great Britain by
PURNELL BOOK PRODUCTION LIMITED
A MEMBER OF BPCC plc